My Secret Unicorn

Starlight Surprise

Touching her heels to Twilight's sides, Lauren rode him down the overgrown path. As they got nearer, the tree house seemed to loom up in front of them. Its old grey walls were covered with green moss and the air around it seemed still and silent. A shiver ran down Lauren's spine. It did look kind of spooky. Her heart started to beat faster. It couldn't really be haunted, could it?

Books in the series

My Secret Unicorn

Starlight Surprise

Linda Chapman

Illustrated by Biz Hull

PUFFIN

PUFFIN BOOKS

UK | USA | Canada | Ireland | Australia
India | New Zealand | South Africa

Puffin Books is part of the Penguin Random House group of companies
whose addresses can be found at global.penguinrandomhouse.com.

www.penguin.co.uk   www.puffin.co.uk   www.ladybird.co.uk

First published 2003
This edition published 2018

005

Written by Linda Chapman
Text copyright © Working Partners Ltd, 2003
Illustrations copyright © Biz Hull, 2003
Created by Working Partners Ltd, London W6 0QT

The moral right of the author and illustrator has been asserted

Typeset in 14.25/21.5 pt Bembo
Printed in Great Britain by Clays Ltd, Elcograf S.p.A.

A CIP catalogue record for this book is available from the British Library

ISBN: 978–0–241–36919–7

All correspondence to:
Puffin Books
Penguin Random House Children's
80 Strand, London WC2R 0RL

To my parents, for everything ★

CHAPTER

One

'Faster, Twilight! Faster!' Lauren Foster cried, burying her hands in Twilight's soft mane.

With a whinny, Twilight surged forward. Lauren's light-brown hair blew back behind her and she laughed out loud as Twilight swooped through the night air, the moonlight shining on his silvery horn.

Lauren loved these moments – the secret times when Twilight, her pony, changed into a magical flying unicorn.

'This is fun!' Twilight exclaimed.

'It sure is!' Lauren agreed as the wind whipped her cheeks. Far below, she could see the treetops and farmhouse where she lived with her mum, dad and younger brother, Max. Her family didn't know about Twilight's secret. In fact, right now, they thought she was in the paddock giving Twilight his evening feed. Lauren smiled as she imagined how amazed they would be if they could see her flying through the moonlit sky instead.

Suddenly Twilight pricked up his ears. 'Hey, listen – what's that noise?' he asked.

Lauren heard a frightened bleating
sound.

'It's coming from the woods,' Twilight
decided. 'It sounds like an animal in
trouble.'

'Let's go and see what it is,' Lauren said immediately.

Twilight cantered down among the trees.

As they got lower, Lauren saw a young fawn caught in a thicket of brambles.

'Oh, look!' she cried. 'The poor thing's all tangled up.'

The thorns were caught in the fawn's russet-red coat and a wiry branch had wrapped itself around one of his legs. No matter how the baby deer struggled, he couldn't get free. His mother watched anxiously from nearby. Seeing Twilight landing on the grass, she shied back in panic. The fawn redoubled his efforts to break free, stamping his hooves in terror.

'We *have* to help him,' Lauren said
determinedly.

Twilight nodded and approached the
fawn. With a quiet whicker, he touched
his horn gently against the fawn's neck.
In moments, the terror magically ebbed
from the deer's eyes. He stopped
struggling and stood still.

Lauren dismounted. Ignoring the
thorns that grabbed and tore at her bare
hands, she crouched down and began to
pull the wiry bramble from around the
fawn's leg.

'There you are, baby,' she said at last.
'You're free now.'

Twilight lifted his horn from the
fawn's neck and used it to sweep aside

the brambles. With a snort, the fawn leapt out of the thicket and ran to his mother's side.

The two deer looked at Twilight in astonishment, then bounded away into the forest.

'It doesn't matter that they've seen

you, does it?' Lauren asked Twilight as she picked her way out of the brambles.

Twilight shook his head. 'Most animals know that a unicorn's secret must be kept. It's other people who must never be allowed to find out about me in case they try to use my magic for bad things.'

Lauren put her arm over Twilight's neck. There was a warm glow in her heart. 'I'm glad we were here to help.'

'Me too,' Twilight agreed. He nuzzled her hands. 'But you've hurt yourself,' he said with concern.

Lauren looked at the deep scratches on her hands. She shrugged. 'It was worth it.'

Twilight bent his head and his horn gently touched Lauren's scratches.

Warmth seemed to flood over Lauren's hands and she gasped. The scratches tingled sharply for a few seconds and then all of a sudden the pain disappeared. Lauren stared. Where the wounds had been, there were just some faint pink marks. 'Wow!' she said, looking at Twilight in amazement. 'I didn't know you could do that!'

'Me neither,' Twilight said, looking equally surprised.

'It must be unicorn magic,' Lauren said.

Twilight nodded. Unicorns had many magical powers but neither he nor Lauren knew what they all were yet. Ever since Lauren had first changed him into a unicorn they had been finding out what his powers were.

Taking hold of his mane, Lauren swung herself up on to his back. 'We should go home. If I'm gone too long, Mum or Dad will come outside to find out what I'm doing. We mustn't risk them seeing you.'

With one push of his powerful hind

legs, Twilight kicked up into the sky and they headed back to Granger's Farm.

As they landed in Twilight's paddock, Lauren hugged him. 'I'm going to keep you forever,' she told him happily as she dismounted. 'We'll always live here,' she went on, looking around at the fields and outbuildings of her parents' new farm, 'and if I ever have kids, they can learn to ride on you and they'll believe in unicorns too!' But then a worrying thought struck her. 'How . . . how long do unicorns live, Twilight?'

Twilight looked puzzled. 'I'm not sure.' He snorted. 'I don't really know much about being a unicorn. I left the land

where I was born when I was a young
foal and I haven't met any other unicorns
since.'

'We must find out,' Lauren told him.

Twilight looked thoughtful. 'I bet Mrs
Fontana would know.'

Lauren nodded. Mrs Fontana was an
old lady who owned a second-hand
bookshop and the only other person who
knew about Twilight. She too had found
a unicorn when she was a young girl.
When Lauren had first got Twilight, Mrs
Fontana had given her a book about
unicorns that had contained the spell she
needed to turn Twilight into his magical
form. 'I'll ask her next time I see her,'
Lauren said.

She looked towards the lights of the farmhouse. They seemed very bright in the darkness. It was getting late. 'I should go in,' she said. Giving Twilight a pat, she said the words that would turn him back into a pony.

'*Twilight Star, Twilight Star,*
Twinkling high above so far,
Protect this secret from prying eyes
And return my unicorn to his disguise.
His magical shape is for my eyes only,
Let him be once more a pony.'

There was a purple flash and then Twilight was standing there – no longer a unicorn but a rather shaggy thirteen-hand grey pony.

He lifted his muzzle to her face. Lauren kissed his soft nose. 'See you tomorrow, Twilight,' she whispered. Then she turned and hurried to the house.

CHAPTER

Two

When Lauren went down for breakfast the next morning, she found her mum and Max already up. Her brother was sitting on their mother's knee. Lauren stared. Now that Max was six, he almost never sat on their mum's knee.

'Bad dream,' Mrs Foster mouthed to Lauren over Max's curly dark head.

Lauren nodded understandingly and,

patting Buddy, Max's Bernese mountain dog puppy who was sitting beside the table, she sat down.

'Lauren,' Max said slowly, as Lauren poured herself some cereal. 'Do you believe in ghosts?'

'No,' Lauren said, looking at him in surprise. 'Why?'

'Because there's a tree house by the creek that everyone says is haunted,' Max replied.

Mrs Foster frowned. 'Is this what your bad dream was about, Max?'

Max nodded.

'But, honey,' Mrs Foster said, turning him so she could see his face, 'ghosts don't exist.'

'But Matthew and David say they saw one,' Max said. 'It was white and it floated through the air above the tree house *and* it made noises.' He looked scared.

'Oh, Max,' Mrs Foster said. 'It was probably a bird. They just *thought* it was a ghost.'

'Yeah, Mum's right. There are no such things as ghosts, Max,' Lauren said, backing her mum up.

But Max didn't look convinced.

'Do you want to go for a ride in the woods after school, Lauren?' asked Mel, one of Lauren's friends. They were leaving the classroom at morning break.

'Definitely,' Lauren replied.

Jessica, their other friend, sighed longingly. 'I wish I had my pony. Then I could come too,' she said. Jessica's dad had promised to buy her a pony in the summer holidays, but that was still ages away.

'You can still come,' Lauren said, not wanting Jessica to feel left out. 'Bring your bike and we can swap. You can ride Twilight some of the time while I ride your bike.'

Jessica's face lit up. 'That would be great!'

Just then, three boys from another class came running down the corridor. They barged past, bumping into Jessica so that she stumbled and fell over. 'Hey!' Lauren

called angrily as they ran on, laughing,
not even bothering to stop and see if
Jessica was OK.

'Ow!' Jessica said, picking herself up off the floor.

'Idiots!' Lauren said, staring after the boys.

Mel nodded. 'It was Nick, Dan and Andrew – Nick's the tall one, Dan's the one with the freckles and Andrew's got the curly hair. They're in my cousin Katie's class. She says they're really mean.'

'Well, she's obviously right,' Lauren said. She hadn't come across the three boys before. Her family had only moved into Granger's Farm recently, and she didn't know everyone at her new school yet.

The three girls started talking again about the ride they were going to go on that afternoon. 'It's so hot – we could visit the creek,' Mel suggested.

'Yeah,' Jessica agreed. 'Shadow and Twilight can go in the water – they'll like that.'

Lauren thought about Silver Creek, the small river that wound its way down from the mountains, through the woods, and remembered the conversation over breakfast. 'You'll never guess what Max said this morning,' she told them with a grin. 'He said that there's a tree house near the creek that's haunted!'

To her surprise, Mel and Jessica didn't grin back.

'Yeah, we know,' Mel said seriously.

'It's up a little path away from the

creek,' Jessica said. 'It's totally spooky.'

Lauren stared at them. 'It can't be haunted, surely?'

Mel's shoulder-length curls bounced as she nodded quickly. 'Jen and Sarah went near it a while back and they said they saw a ghost in the trees!'

'Really?' Lauren said, her eyes widening, as she remembered that Max's friends had told him the same thing.

'But there are loads of other trails that lead to the creek,' Jessica said quickly. 'We don't have to go near the tree house.'

Mel shivered. 'I wouldn't go near it if you paid me a hundred dollars.'

'Me neither,' Jessica agreed.

Lauren didn't know what to say. She

didn't believe in ghosts but Mel and
Jessica seemed genuinely scared. What *was*
this tree house like?

After school, Lauren groomed Twilight.
As she worked she told him about the
ride to the creek. 'It will be lovely,' she
said, stopping to wipe her arm across her
hot forehead. 'You'll be able to go into
the water to paddle and drink.'

Twilight nuzzled her shoulder.
Although he couldn't talk back when he
was in his pony form, Lauren knew that
he understood every word she said.

Just then, Max came running down
the path from the house. He seemed to
have forgotten about his nightmare and

was his usual happy, boisterous self. 'Hi, Lauren!' he shouted.

'Where's Buddy?' Lauren asked, surprised to see Max without his puppy.

'Inside,' Max told her, stopping near Twilight and patting him. 'He just wants to lie down. Mum says it's too hot for him outside.'

'Poor Buddy,' Lauren said, thinking of the puppy's thick black fur. 'I bet he wishes he could take his coat off when the weather's like this.'

Max nodded. 'Are you going out for a ride?' he asked.

Lauren nodded. 'I'm going to the creek with Mel and Jessica.'

'Can I come?' Max said.

Lauren hesitated. She really wanted to go with just her friends, but it wouldn't be very nice for Max to be stuck at home on his own.

'*Pleeease*,' Max begged.

'OK,' Lauren agreed. 'You can come on your bike – if Mum says it's all right.'

'Cool!' Max said. 'I'll go and ask.' He turned to run back up the path and then stopped. 'You're not going near that haunted tree house, are you?' he asked, suddenly looking anxious.

Lauren saw the worry in his eyes. 'No, don't worry, we won't,' she said. 'Though there's nothing to be scared of anyway. Ghosts don't exist, you know.'

'I bet they do,' Max said.

'Well, I bet they don't,' Lauren said firmly. She took Twilight's bridle off the fence. 'Now, are you going to ask Mum if you can come? Or shall I go without you?'

'Hold on! I'll go and ask!' Max said, turning to run up the path.

A little while later, Lauren, Mel, Jessica and Max made their way down through the shady woods to Silver Creek. Jessica and Max were cycling ahead on their bikes, while Lauren and Mel rode behind. Occasionally, Twilight would touch noses with Mel's dapple-grey pony, Shadow, as they walked. The two ponies were very good friends.

'This is fun,' Lauren said happily to Mel, as they rode along the sandy trail. Mel nodded and Lauren called out, 'Jessica! Wait and we'll swap – you can ride Twilight the rest of the way to the creek.'

'And you can share Shadow with me on the way back,' Mel offered.

Jessica and Max waited for them to catch up.

Lauren halted Twilight. 'Why don't we go down that track?' she said, nodding towards a small overgrown path that headed off the main trail in the direction of the creek. 'It looks like a short cut.'

'It is,' Mel said, 'but we can't go down there. It goes past the tree house.'

Lauren saw Max gulp. She looked
down the shadowy track with its canopy
of overhanging trees and saw a tree house
up in the branches of an oak tree. It was
made of wood and had windows and a
roof. It looked as if it would be a
wonderful place for a den – from inside
you'd be able to see all around. 'It doesn't
look haunted to me,' she said.

'Well, it is,' Jessica said. 'And there's no
way I'm going down there.'

Max started pushing his bike away
from the path. He looked frightened. 'I
don't like it here, Lauren. I think there
are ghosts.'

'There aren't,' Lauren told him.

Twilight stepped towards the path. His

ears were pricked up and Lauren took
courage. If Twilight wasn't scared, then
why should she be? She had an idea.
'Watch,' she said to Max. 'I'm going to
ride to the tree house and back, just to
prove there aren't any ghosts there.'

'Lauren! No!' Mel and Jessica
exclaimed.

Lauren ignored them. Touching her
heels to Twilight's sides, she rode him
down the overgrown path. As they got
nearer, the tree house seemed to loom up
in front of them. Its old grey walls were
covered with green moss and the air
around it seemed still and silent. A shiver
ran down Lauren's spine. It did look kind
of spooky. Her heart started to beat faster.

It couldn't really be haunted, could it?

Seeming to sense her sudden nervousness, Twilight hesitated, his ears flicking back uncertainly.

'Walk on, boy,' Lauren encouraged, but her voice shook slightly. They were very close to the tree house now. She took a deep breath. Just a few more paces and then she'd be able to turn round and Max would see that there was nothing to be frightened of.

'Whooo-aaaaaooooo.' A low noise suddenly groaned through the quiet air.

CHAPTER

Three

Lauren gasped. Twilight stopped dead. The noise was coming from the tree house!

Suddenly something exploded out of the bushes in front of them.

For a moment, all Lauren could see was Twilight's grey mane and neck as he reared in surprise. Behind her, she heard screams. She cried out in alarm, but as

Twilight landed,
her cry turned to
a gasp of relief.
A cat was
streaking
away through
the trees, its ears
flat and its long brown tail flying out
behind it.

Lauren laughed shakily and patted
Twilight's neck. 'It was just a cat,' she said.
She turned in the saddle. Mel, Jessica and
Max were looking rather sheepish.

'I almost fainted with fright,' Jessica
called, as Lauren rode back towards them.

'Me too,' Mel said. 'I was sure it was a
ghost.'

'It could have been a ghost cat,' Max
put in, looking warily into the trees.

'Max,' Lauren said, getting off Twilight,
'how many times do I have to tell you,
there are no such things as ghosts!'

But as she held the stirrup so that
Jessica could mount, she felt a flicker of
doubt. The tree house really had looked
very creepy . . . and what about that
noise? It hadn't sounded like any animal
or bird Lauren had ever heard. Deciding
not to say anything about it in case Max
got even more scared, Lauren picked up
Jessica's bike.

'You were really brave, Lauren,' Max
said, looking at her with respect, as they
cycled on ahead of Mel and Jessica.

'There wasn't anything to be scared of,' Lauren told him as firmly as she could. As his bike wobbled over a tree root, she caught sight of something blue sticking out of the bag on the back of his bike. 'Is that Donkey?' she said in surprise.

Donkey was Max's oldest stuffed toy. He was a faded dark-blue colour with droopy ears. When Max had been little he had taken Donkey everywhere with him, but in the last year he had started to say that Donkey was babyish. Although, as Mrs Foster had told Lauren, this didn't stop Max from taking Donkey to bed with him each night.

Max looked round and, when he saw

Donkey's leg sticking out of his bike bag,
his cheeks turned pink. 'I didn't put him
there,' he said defensively. Quickly he
stopped and pushed Donkey into the
bag. 'Only little kids have cuddly toys.'

Standing up on his pedals, he rode on.

Lauren smiled to herself. Max would never admit it, but she had a feeling that he had brought Donkey along with him just in case they met any ghosts.

They turned down the track that led to the creek. Lauren was warm from cycling and couldn't wait to take her trainers off to wade in the cool water. There were several people there already – some sitting on the grassy banks, others splashing in the sparkling creek.

'Let's go down to the left where it's less busy,' Mel called. They rode to a quiet spot and dismounted from the bikes and ponies.

'Thanks for letting me ride Twilight,'

Jessica said, dismounting. She helped
Lauren run up the stirrups and loosen
Twilight's girth, and then Lauren led
him down to the water.

Twilight walked in up to his knees
and buried his muzzle in the creek. As
he drank the cool, fresh water, Lauren
thought about that evening when they
would go flying through the sky.

After Twilight had been for a paddle,
Lauren led him out of the river and
tied him up to graze with Shadow.
Then she sat down to take her trainers
off. Mel, Jessica and Max were already
down at the water's edge. Leaving her
shoes beside theirs, Lauren went to
join them.

Jessica had brought a ball and they threw it to one another. Then they took it in turns to try skimming stones across the surface of the water.

'This is great,' Max said, turning a smiling face to Lauren's as he hunted for a flat stone. Behind them, Twilight whinnied.

Lauren glanced round, and saw that the three boys from school who had knocked Jessica over were standing by the pile of shoes. They were nudging each other and laughing. Lauren saw the tallest, strongest one, Nick, reach down and pick up the shoes and pass them to Andrew and Dan. They were going to take them!

'Hey!' Lauren shouted, starting to run up the slope towards them.

The boys looked up but, seeing that it was just Lauren, they stood their ground.

Lauren came to a panting stop. 'Leave our shoes alone!'

Andrew, a stocky boy with close-cropped, curly blond hair, grinned and dangled one of Lauren's trainers from his hands. 'Seems to me like you'd have a hard time getting home without them,' he smirked.

'Give them back!' Lauren said.

To her relief, she heard Mel, Jessica and Max running up behind her. They had realized what was happening. 'Give us our shoes!' Jessica exclaimed.

'You'd better ask nicely,' Dan taunted her.

'Hey, what's that?' Nick said, his sharp eyes spotting Donkey's head sticking out of Max's bike bag. The toy had half fallen out when Max had thrown his bike on the ground. Nick swooped down and grabbed Donkey, hauling him out and holding him by his tail. 'Look! It's a stuffed toy!'

Lauren stiffened as she saw poor old Donkey dangling from Nick's huge hand. Only the fact that Nick was head and shoulders taller than she was stopped her from throwing herself at him. 'Put him down,' she said through gritted teeth.

'Yours, is he?' Nick said. His eyes swept

across the group. 'Or maybe he's yours?'
he sneered at Max.

'He's not mine,' Max said, his face
flushing crimson.

'Just give him back,' Lauren said.

'Make me,' Nick taunted.

Lauren lost her temper. Running
towards Nick, she grabbed at Donkey.

With a whoop of delight, Nick
whipped Donkey out of her reach and
then charged away. 'Come and get him if
you want him!'

Dropping the shoes as they went,
Andrew and Dan raced after him along
the bank. Lauren sprinted after them, the
sight of Donkey bouncing around in
Nick's fist spurring her on.

Suddenly the boys stopped. 'Still want him?' Nick called.

'Yes!' Lauren panted as she reached them, and then she realized where they were standing. Just behind them, a little way up an overgrown track, was the tree house!

'Go and get him then,' Nick laughed. Lifting his arm, he hurled Donkey towards the trees. Laughing loudly, he and the other two boys ran away along the bank of the creek.

Lauren stared in horror as Donkey went spinning up into the blue sky, turning over and over until he landed in the branches of a tree . . . right next to the creepy old tree house.

Four

'Donkey!' Max exclaimed, running up behind Lauren.

'Don't worry,' Lauren said quickly. 'We'll get him down.'

Just then, Mel and Jessica reached them. 'We've got all our shoes,' Mel said. She looked up at the tree. 'Oh.'

'Was he a special toy?' Jessica asked, looking at Max.

Max stared at Donkey for a moment and then he shook his head. 'No,' he said, his voice trembling. 'It's just a silly old thing.' Swinging round, he marched away, but not before Lauren had seen the tears springing to his eyes.

'Max,' Lauren said, going after him and stopping him, 'come on. I'll get Donkey down for you.'

'I don't want him,' Max said angrily, pulling away from her, and he ran down to the creek.

'Maybe we could climb the tree and get it,' Jessica said, joining Lauren. 'But it is very high up.'

'It's OK,' Lauren said quickly, catching Jessica's worried look at the tree house.

'Max says it doesn't matter.' But inside
she was thinking, *Tonight Twilight and I can
fly here. We can get Donkey down.* For a
second, an image of the tree house at
night – dark, spooky, surrounded by trees
– filled her mind, but she forced it away.
She'd be fine with Twilight. They could
just swoop down and get Donkey back
and then fly away.

Feeling happier, she smiled at Mel and
Jessica. They were looking concerned.
'Come on,' she said. 'Let's get back to the
ponies.'

That night, while her mum and dad were
watching a film on TV, Lauren went out
to Twilight's paddock and said the spell

that turned him into a unicorn. There
was a bright purple flash and suddenly
Twilight was standing in front of her – a
snow-white unicorn.

'Hello,' he said, nuzzling her. 'Are we
going to go and get Max's toy?' Lauren
had told him all about her plans for
rescuing Donkey while riding back from
Mel's.

'Definitely,' Lauren replied. She had
heard her mum asking where Donkey
was when Max got into bed that
evening. Max had replied that he didn't
know. He had muttered it as if he didn't
care but Lauren was sure that it did
matter. Although he'd never admit it,
she knew Max loved Donkey almost as

much as he loved Buddy.

Grabbing hold of Twilight's mane, Lauren mounted. 'Let's go.'

Twilight leapt up into the sky. 'Twilight,' Lauren said, 'you don't think the tree house is really haunted, do you?'

'I don't know,' Twilight replied.

As the darkness closed in around them, Lauren felt goosebumps prickle her skin. 'But ghosts don't exist,' she said, trying to convince herself by speaking out loud. 'They're just make believe, like monsters or dragons or . . .' Her voice trailed off.

Or unicorns, she thought. She swallowed, her stomach feeling as if it had just done a loop-the-loop. People said unicorns didn't exist, but they did, didn't they? What if she was wrong about ghosts?

Just then her thoughts were distracted by the sight of someone walking in the woods below. Lauren stiffened in surprise. Normally they didn't come across anyone at night. 'Careful!' she whispered quickly to Twilight. 'Look!'

Twilight started to swoop upwards but, as he did so, Lauren recognized the figure below.

'Mrs Fontana!' she exclaimed. 'What are you doing here?' she asked as Twilight cantered downwards and landed beside the old lady.

Mrs Fontana's bright blue eyes

twinkled. 'Walking Walter, of course,' she
said. She whistled softly and Walter, her
little black and white terrier dog, came
bounding out from the bushes. Twilight
lowered his head in greeting. Trotting

over to the unicorn, Walter licked
Twilight on the nose and woofed, before
going to sit at Mrs Fontana's side.

'He says it is good to see you,' Mrs
Fontana said. Her face creased into what
seemed like a hundred wrinkles as she
smiled. 'And he's right – it is. What are
you both up to tonight?' she asked.

'We're going to get my brother's toy,'
Lauren replied. 'Some boys threw it up
into a tree.'

Mrs Fontana nodded, looking pleased.
'So, you're still doing good things then?'

Lauren nodded. Ever since she had
turned Twilight into a unicorn, they had
been secretly helping several of her
friends overcome problems – although, of

course, her friends knew nothing about the magical side of Twilight. That was the thing about unicorns – they roamed the human world looking just like little grey ponies until they found a Unicorn Friend – a child with enough imagination to believe in magic. Once the Turning Spell had been said and the unicorn had changed into their magical form, then they and their Unicorn Friend worked together, helping others.

'That's as it should be,' Mrs Fontana said. 'My unicorn and I did a lot of good too.'

'What happened to your unicorn?' Lauren asked, remembering her own conversation with Twilight from the night

before. 'Did he . . . did he die?' Her voice
faltered on the words as she imagined
how she would feel if Twilight ever died.
She was relieved when Mrs Fontana
smiled.

'Oh no,' the old lady replied. 'He
returned to Arcadia – like all unicorns
do.'

Lauren and Twilight stared at her, not
quite understanding.

'Unicorns come to this world to carry
out good deeds,' Mrs Fontana explained.
'Then they go back to Arcadia – the
magical world where they were born.
Those unicorns who have been the most
courageous and resourceful earn the right
to become Golden Unicorns, the wise

rulers of Arcadia. That's why you two
have to work out how to use Twilight's
magical powers all by yourselves,' she said.
'It's a test for Twilight – being here. If he
does enough good work, then maybe
he will become a Golden Unicorn
one day.'

Lauren gripped Twilight's mane. He
was going to go away one day? But he
couldn't. He was hers.

Twilight seemed to be thinking the
same thing. He stamped his foot in alarm.
'But I don't want to go back to Arcadia! I
want to stay here with Lauren!'

'One day you will feel differently,' Mrs
Fontana said. 'It is your destiny.' Seeing
the alarm and unhappiness on their faces,

she shook her head in a kindly way. 'Do
not worry about this now. Concentrate
on being here together.' She smiled.

'Now, my dears, I must go. Come, Walter,' she said to the little dog.

Walter leapt to his feet, and he and Mrs Fontana vanished among the trees.

CHAPTER
Five

Silence fell on Lauren and Twilight as they both thought about what it would be like to leave the other.

At last Lauren took a deep, trembling breath. 'We should get Donkey,' she said quietly. 'It's getting late.'

Twilight nodded. Without saying a word, he took off into the sky. But Lauren didn't feel any of the usual joy she felt when flying. At the back of her mind, a thought was trying to turn itself into words. Lauren tried to catch hold of it – she was sure it was important and that it had something to do with what Mrs Fontana had just said.

'We're here,' Twilight announced as they reached the creek. 'We should get Max's toy.'

Lauren took a deep breath and agreed. After all, she and Twilight were supposed to do good, just as Mrs Fontana had said. The old lady's words came back to her: *Unicorns come to this world to carry out good deeds and then they go back to Arcadia.*

The thought that had been hovering vaguely in Lauren's mind suddenly became clear.

'Twilight!' she gasped, as he rose upwards. 'Stop!'

Halfway to the treehouse, Twilight stopped and hovered in the air. 'What is it?'

'Don't you see?' Lauren said. 'The more good we do, the sooner you'll go away.'

'I don't understand,' Twilight said.

'Mrs Fontana said that you were here to pass a test,' Lauren said. 'To pass it you help others with me. That must mean that when we've done enough good deeds, you'll go back to Arcadia.'

Twilight spoke slowly. 'So, you mean the more I help, the sooner the time comes for me to go away?'

'Yes,' Lauren whispered.

There was a long pause.

Lauren looked at Donkey hanging in the tree and bit her lip. 'You know,

maybe Max doesn't really want Donkey
back,' she said suddenly.

He does, a voice inside her head
protested. Lauren tried not to listen to it.

'I mean, he *did* say that he thought
Donkey was babyish,' she went on out
loud, 'and that he didn't want him any
more.'

Her mind filled with a picture of
Max's face when he had first seen
Donkey in the tree. She pushed it away.

'And he's right,' she went on. 'It is kind
of babyish for a six-year-old to still take a
cuddly animal to bed.'

'So, you think that maybe we *shouldn't*
get the toy,' Twilight said hesitantly.

'Yes,' Lauren said. A horrid guilty

feeling was welling up inside her, but she ignored it. 'Let's leave Donkey here.'

'Are you sure?' Twilight asked.

'Definitely,' Lauren said. 'Let's go home.'

But inside she was far from sure.

They flew back to Granger's Farm in silence.

'Goodnight,' Lauren said, after she'd changed Twilight back into a pony. 'I'll see you in the morning.'

Twilight nodded, but Lauren was sure his eyes looked troubled.

We've done the right thing, Lauren told herself as she walked back to the house. *Max didn't really want Donkey.*

And you didn't want to do a good deed

*with Twilight in case it brought him closer to
going away,* the little voice in her head
said.

'That's not true,' Lauren said aloud,
wishing that the little voice would leave
her alone.

On the way up to her bedroom, she
looked into the lounge where her mum
was reading and her dad was watching
the TV.

'I'm going up to bed,' she said.

Her dad looked at the clock on the
wall. 'Have you been with Twilight all this
time?' he asked in surprise.

'Yes,' Lauren replied.

'But it's dark outside,' her mum said.
'What have you been doing?'

Lauren shrugged vaguely. 'Talking to him – this and that.'

Her dad shook his head. 'You know, I thought that maybe you'd lose interest in ponies once you had one of your own, Lauren Foster. But you've sure proved me wrong.'

Her mum smiled. 'You really love that pony, don't you, Lauren?'

Lauren nodded. 'Yes,' she said, 'I do.' She imagined Twilight leaving her and her heart felt as if it was going to break.

Feeling tears spring to her eyes, she rubbed her hand across her face, pretending that she was tired so that her mum and dad wouldn't see. Her mum came over and kissed her. 'You look exhausted, honey. Go and get ready for bed. I'll be up shortly to say goodnight.'

Lauren didn't sleep well that night. She tossed and turned in her bed – one minute thinking about Twilight going away, and the next thinking about Donkey still hanging in the tree.

She woke up early and got dressed. On the way downstairs she passed Max's room. Max wasn't in his bed. Wondering where he was, Lauren carried on. The door to her mum and dad's room was open and when Lauren looked in she saw that Max was in their parents' bed. Her dad had already got up and had

started work on the farm. Lauren
stopped in the doorway.

Mrs Foster opened her eyes. 'Hi, there,'
she said, sitting up in bed. She glanced at
the bedside clock. 'You're up early.'

'I was having bad dreams,' Lauren told
her.

'Not you as well,' Mrs Foster said,
yawning. 'Max had another nightmare last
night too.'

Just then Max woke up. 'Mummy?'

'I'm here,' Mrs Foster said, kissing his
dark head.

'I like sleeping in your bed,' Max said
to her, cuddling closer.

'Well, I'm afraid that tonight it's back
to your own bed,' Mrs Foster said.

'There's hardly any space for your dad
and me with you in here as well.'

'But my bed's lonely,' Max said.

Mrs Foster ruffled his hair. 'It won't be

when we find Donkey. I'll have a look for him today.'

Max's eyes met Lauren's. *So*, she realized, *he hasn't told Mum where Donkey really is.*

'I don't need Donkey,' Max muttered.

'Well, maybe I'll try and find him anyway,' Mrs Foster said, smiling at Lauren.

Max saw the smile and threw the covers back. 'You won't be able to,' he said, getting up. 'And, anyway, it doesn't matter. I told you – I don't care.' But as he pushed past Lauren, she saw the unhappiness in his eyes.

Lauren felt dreadful all day. *I should have*

got Donkey down from the tree for Max, she thought as she stared unseeingly at a page of sums at school. It was just . . .

She swallowed as she admitted the truth. It was just that if she and Twilight did good deeds, then Twilight would have to leave her.

Mel leaned over. 'You OK, Lauren?' she asked.

'I'm fine,' Lauren said, trying to smile.

But inside, she knew that she wasn't fine at all.

CHAPTER

Six

'I don't want to go to bed,' Max said, clinging to Mrs Foster's arm that evening when she suggested that it was his bedtime. 'Can't I stay up – please, Mum?'

'No,' Mrs Foster said, looking at his pale face. 'You look worn out. Come on – upstairs with you. You can snuggle down in bed and I'll read you a story.'

Max hung back. Mrs Foster crouched
down beside him. 'Hey, how about just
for one night, we let Buddy sleep in your
room with you?' she said. 'Will that make
you feel better?'

Max nodded. 'Yes.'

'OK then,' Mrs Foster said kindly. 'Just this once. Come on, Buddy,' she said to the puppy, who was stretched out on the floor in front of the sofa. 'You can come upstairs.'

Buddy leapt to his feet. Wagging his tail, he bounded towards the door, stopping to give Max a slobbery lick on the way. Looking a bit happier, Max headed for the stairs with Mrs Foster.

Lauren followed them. Sitting down in her room to do her homework, she could hear her mum settling Max in his bed and starting to read to him.

Mrs Foster read on for what seemed a long time. It wasn't until Lauren had started on the last of her homework –

spellings – that she heard her mum turn
the light off and quietly leave Max's
room.

'Mum!' It was Max's voice.

Through her half-open door, Lauren
saw her mum pause in Max's doorway,
her face looking tired. 'Yes, Max?'

'I . . .' Max seemed to be struggling
with the words. 'I want Donkey.'

Lauren's heart clenched.

'I'm sorry, honey,' Mrs Foster said
gently. 'But I just don't know where he
is. Cuddle your other toys instead. We can
have another look in the morning.'

She waited a moment by the door.
When Max said no more, she turned and
went downstairs.

Lauren looked at the printed column of spellings in her school book with its red and gold logo, but she couldn't concentrate on them. After a while, she went to her brother's bedroom. 'Max?' she whispered. There was no answer. Maybe he'd fallen asleep.

Lauren pushed the door open. 'Max?' she whispered again.

And then she heard the sound of Max crying quietly.

'Oh, Max!' Lauren exclaimed. She ran to his bed. Max was lying face down, crying into his pillow. Buddy was sitting beside him, whimpering anxiously. Crouching down, Lauren put her arms round her little brother. 'Max, please

don't cry.'

Through the darkness, Max lifted a
tear-stained face to hers. 'I miss Donkey,
Lauren.'

The words tumbled out of Lauren. 'I'll

get him for you,' she said.

Max sat up in bed and stroked Buddy's head. 'You can't. He's too high up in that tree and it's right by the haunted tree house.' He gulped and Buddy reached up to lick the salty tears from his cheeks with his pink tongue. 'He's gone forever.'

'He hasn't,' Lauren told him. 'I'll get him. I promise.'

'Really?' Max said, a faint light of hope glimmering in his eyes.

Lauren nodded. 'Really,' she answered.

Leaving Max with Buddy, Lauren went downstairs. 'I'm just going to see Twilight,' she said to her mum and dad, who were in the kitchen.

'Don't be out too long,' her dad said. 'It'll be dark soon.'

'Have you done your homework?' Mrs Foster asked.

Lauren nodded. She still had the spellings to learn but she could look over them the next morning.

'OK then,' her mum said.

Lauren pulled on her trainers and hurried outside. As she reached the path that led to Twilight's paddock, she started to run.

Hearing the sound of her footsteps, Twilight came trotting to the gate.

'Twilight,' Lauren said quickly. 'We've got to go out flying.'

Twilight whinnied and Lauren said the

words of the Turning Spell.

'What's happened?' he asked.

'Max is really upset about Donkey,'
Lauren said. 'He can't sleep. I feel awful.'
She stepped forward and stroked his
neck. 'Twilight, even if it does mean that
it brings the time closer when you have
to go away, we've got to get Donkey
back. I just can't let my brother be so
upset.'

'Of course you can't,' Twilight said.
'We must help.' He shook his mane. 'It
was strange yesterday when we didn't get
Max's toy. It somehow felt wrong. But
this,' he nuzzled her, 'this feels right.'

'I know,' Lauren replied with a smile.

★

They flew to
the creek
and landed
on the
grassy bank.
Donkey was still hanging in
the branches of the tree. It was
getting dark. Lauren's eyes moved to the
nearby tree house. It looked shadowy and
menacing in the gloom. She remembered
the noise she had heard as she had ridden
up to it the day before and suddenly she
felt afraid. What if it really was haunted?
She and Twilight were going to have to
fly right beside it to get Donkey.

Trying not to feel scared, Lauren
patted Twilight's neck. 'OK,' she

whispered. 'Let's fly up.'

Twilight leapt upwards. Lauren's heart was pounding but she felt strong – she knew she was doing the right thing. As Twilight reached the branches where Donkey was hanging, he stopped and hovered in the air. Untangling Donkey's woolly mane and tail from the branches, Lauren took him safely into her arms.

'I've got him!' she cried.

Twilight flew on upwards. As they rose up past the tree house, Lauren even felt brave enough to look in through the windows. The moon was shining through one of them, lighting up the inside of the wooden house. There was nothing there. It was empty. Well, apart

from some rubbish on the wooden
floorboards – chocolate wrappers, empty
cans, a comic and a . . .

'Twilight – stop,' Lauren said suddenly.

'What's the matter?' Twilight asked.

'Can you take me close to one of the
windows, please?' Lauren asked.

'Sure.' Twilight did as she asked. Lauren
looked in again. Yes, there on the floor of
the tree house was a school spelling book
with a red and gold logo. It was from
Lauren's school! But what was it doing in
the tree house?

She also realized that the rubbish on
the floor looked new. The discarded
wrappers were still bright and colourful
and the comic was the latest issue of

Spider-man – Lauren had seen some of
the kids in her class reading similar copies
only the day before.

But who would have been in the tree
house? Everyone was scared of it.

Lauren looked at the spelling book
again and made up her mind. 'I have to
go inside,' she said to Twilight.

'OK,' Twilight said, flying as close to
the window as he could.

The wood of the tree house was old
but solid. As Lauren grabbed hold of the
window sill and pulled herself over it,
she found herself thinking again that it
would make a wonderful den. It was so
lovely up in the tree and in the daytime
you must be able to see all around.

She saw something white in one corner and stopped. It looked like a pile of cotton sheets. Her skin prickled. What if there was something under them?

Taking a deep breath, she crept over and touched the edge of the sheet with the toe of her trainer. Nothing moved. Lauren moved the top sheet. Underneath it there were two more sheets, a toy microphone and a long stick.

Lauren frowned and picked up the microphone. Max had one like it at home. It made your voice sound strange and echoey when you spoke into it. But what was it doing here?

She walked over to the school book and opened it curiously. Who did it belong to?

A name was written inside.

Lauren gasped. *Nick Snyder.* He was the
boy who had thrown Donkey into the
tree. But what had he been doing in the
tree house?

Her eyes widened. There was only one explanation. 'Twilight,' she said, hurrying to the window. 'I think the boys who threw Donkey into the tree are trying to pretend the place is haunted!'

'What?' Twilight snorted in surprise.

'There's a school book on the floor that belongs to one of them,' Lauren told him quickly. 'So they must have been here. There are some sheets and a stick. You could hang the sheets on a stick and wave them high up in the branches to make people think they've seen ghosts. There's also a toy microphone. I bet the boys have been using it to make that spooky noise we heard.'

'But why would they do that?'

Twilight asked in astonishment.

'I don't know,' Lauren said. She started to climb over the window ledge and on to his back. 'But I think we should try to find out.'

Seven

As Lauren went up to her bedroom, she stopped by Max's door. 'Max,' she said softly.

There was only the sound of Max's breathing. He had finally fallen asleep.

Lauren went quietly into the room. Buddy was lying beside the bed. He thumped his tail on the floor when he saw Lauren, but he didn't get up.

Lauren tucked Donkey under Max's arm. ''Night, Buddy,' she whispered and then, with a smile, she crept out of the room.

At six o'clock in the morning, Max came flying into her room with Donkey in his arms. 'Lauren!' he cried, jumping on to her bed and waking her with a start. 'You got Donkey back for me!'

Lauren grinned. 'I told you I would.'

'But how?' Max said.

Lauren decided it was best to tell him part of the truth. She lowered her voice. 'I used magic,' she whispered.

Max didn't quite seem able to decide whether to believe her. 'Really?'

Lauren nodded.

'Wow!' Max gasped, his eyes widening.

'But you can't tell anyone,' Lauren whispered quickly. 'If Mum asks where Donkey was, just tell her that you found him under the bed or something.'

'OK,' Max agreed eagerly. He sat down on the bed. 'What sort of magic was it, Lauren?'

'I can't tell you,' Lauren smiled. 'It's a secret kind of magic.'

'Please tell me,' Max begged.

Lauren shook her head.

'But . . .'

'Max!' Lauren exclaimed and, picking up one of the cuddly toys from the end of her bed, she hit him with it. 'I said it's a secret!'

Max hit her back with Donkey and the next minute they were in the middle of a toy fight, gasping with laughter as they fell about on Lauren's bed.

At school that day, Lauren watched Nick and his friends. During break they hung out together, muscling in on a game that some of the younger kids were playing.

Lauren frowned as she watched them. They were so mean.

As she and her mum and Max drove home from school that afternoon, Lauren saw Nick and his friends cycling along the pavement. They were pedalling fast, weaving in and out through the other children. As Lauren watched, they turned down a path that led in the direction of the creek. *And,* Lauren thought, *towards the tree house.*

As soon as Lauren got home, she groomed and saddled Twilight. 'We have to go to the tree house,' she told him. 'I want to see if Nick and his friends are there. But they mustn't see us.'

As they set off into the woods, Twilight pulled eagerly at his bit and Lauren let him trot along the sandy trail. As she rode, she wondered how she could get close to the tree house without the boys seeing.

Suddenly Twilight stopped. He was looking down a little overgrown path to the right, as if he wanted to go that way.

'No, Twilight,' Lauren said. 'We're
going to the tree house.'

Twilight stamped his foot.

Lauren frowned. Was he trying to tell
her something?

'You think we should go down here?
Does this lead to the tree house?'

Twilight nodded.

Lauren touched her heels to his sides
and he walked quickly down the path.
After a little way, it forked. Lauren left the
reins loose on Twilight's neck and he
took the right-hand path. They walked
on for a minute more, with Lauren
dodging the low overhanging branches.
Then Twilight came to a halt.

Looking straight ahead, he whickered softly.

Lauren stared. The tree house was just ahead of them, half hidden by trees. If she got off and crawled through the undergrowth she could get to it without having to go down one of the main paths – she could see what the boys were doing without being noticed.

'Clever boy,' she breathed, giving Twilight a hug.

Twilight snorted. Lauren dismounted and began to creep through the thick green undergrowth towards the tree house.

As she got closer she could hear the sound of low voices. Her heart started to thump loudly in her chest. What if the boys saw her? What would they do? She pressed on, trying to ignore the fact that the palms of her hands were starting to sweat.

'It's going to be so cool, staying here tonight,' she heard one of the boys say. *Andrew*, she thought.

Stopping, she crouched behind a bush and listened hard.

'Really cool,' she heard Nick reply. 'We can bring food with us and have a midnight feast.'

Dan laughed. 'Can you imagine how scared everyone else at school would be of staying here overnight?'

'They are so sure it's haunted,'

Andrew said.

'Hey, I hear somebody coming!' Dan said suddenly. 'On the left.'

Lauren froze as for one horrible moment she thought they meant her. But then to her relief she heard the sound of them moving to the far side of the tree house.

'Two girls,' she heard Andrew say.

Nick laughed. 'Come on, guys, into positions.'

Lauren peered out from round the bush. She could just make out two girls, who looked about seven years old, walking rather nervously along the trail that led from the creek past the tree house.

'Go on – I dare you to touch the tree,'
one of them said to the other.

'Sure,' she heard the other reply rather
nervously. 'But it's not really haunted.'

And then, seemingly from the air,
came a disembodied groaning noise.
Lauren knew exactly what was making
the noise – one of the boys with the toy

microphone. She could have laughed out loud at how simple it was, but it wasn't funny.

The two girls screamed and raced back to the creek.

From the tree house came the muffled sounds of laughter.

'That was great!' Lauren heard Dan say.

'They were so scared,' Nick said. 'It's perfect. If I hadn't thought of this, then we'd have had to share this place.'

He sounded very pleased with himself and Lauren felt a wave of anger. Little kids were having nightmares about ghosts and it was all because three boys were too selfish to share the tree house. It was only the thought that the three of them were so much bigger than she was that stopped her from climbing up there and telling them what she thought of them.

Instead, she crawled back to Twilight.

She didn't say anything until they had moved out of sight of the tree house, and then she told him what she had heard.

'Can you believe them?' she demanded indignantly. 'Of all the dumb things to do!' Twilight shook his head. Lauren longed for him to be able to answer back but she couldn't risk turning him into a unicorn in broad daylight in case someone saw. Instead, she stroked his neck. 'We've got to do something about them.'

She thought hard. The question was —
what?

After supper, Lauren left the house and,
in the gathering dusk, turned Twilight
into a unicorn.

'What are we going to do about those
boys?' Twilight said immediately.

'I don't know,' Lauren said. She'd been
wracking her brains.

'We should scare them just like they've
been scaring everyone else,' Twilight said.

'But how?' Lauren asked.

'I'm not sure,' Twilight admitted with a
snort.

Lauren remembered a bit of the boys'
conversation. 'They said they were going

to stay at the tree house tonight. Let's go there now. Maybe we could make noises in the bushes or something – that might scare them.' She wasn't convinced it would work but she desperately wanted to do something, and fast.

Twilight nodded. Lauren climbed on to his back and they cantered away into the sky.

To Lauren's surprise, the tree house was quiet when they arrived. 'They're not here yet,' she said.

'Listen,' Twilight said. 'They're coming.'

Lauren heard the sound of the boys running along the path from the creek.

'Let's fly higher!' she said quickly.

'They mustn't see us.'

As Twilight rose into the sky, Nick and Andrew came running along the path. They were clutching several bags of sweets and bars of chocolate. Dan was a little way behind, carrying a large bag of drinks cans.

'Wait!' he was saying. 'These drinks are heavy!'

'Come on!' Nick called to Andrew. 'Let's eat everything before Dan gets here!' He shouted it loud enough for Dan to hear.

'Hey!' Dan shouted in protest. 'Wait! That's not fair!'

Nick and Andrew reached the rope ladder. Nick climbed into the tree house

first while Andrew waited. Then Andrew
passed the food and scrambled up the
ladder himself.

Watching from above, Lauren saw

Nick whisper something to Andrew. They both grinned and started to haul up the ladder.

The last rung had just disappeared into the tree house when Dan came panting up the path. 'Put the ladder back down!'

Nick and Andrew looked out, grinning. 'Not till we've eaten all the food!' Nick said.

Then he and Andrew disappeared back into the tree house.

Dan shouted out angrily. 'Come on, guys. Stop messing around. Let me in!'

Neither Nick nor Andrew appeared and it seemed as if they were going to eat all the chocolate and crisps themselves.

Dan looked around. It was getting

darker by the second and Lauren saw an
alarmed expression cross his face. An owl
hooted overhead and she saw him jump.
'This isn't funny any more,' he shouted
up to the boys in the tree house. 'Let
me in.'

Nick's voice floated out through the
windows. 'Scared of the ghosts?' he called.
And he and Andrew cracked up laughing.

His words gave Lauren an idea.
'Twilight! This is our chance!' she said.
'Let's swoop down and frighten Dan.
Make yourself look fierce – point your
horn at him.'

'You mean, let him see me?' Twilight
said in astonishment.

'It's dark. He's alone. No one will

believe him if he says he's seen a
unicorn.' Lauren knew it was risky but
she had a feeling it would work. If they
could frighten Dan, then maybe they
could frighten the other two as well.
'Come on!' she said, grabbing his mane.
'Let's go for it!'

Eight

With a great whinny, Twilight plunged down from the sky. He galloped through the air towards Dan, his horn pointing at the boy, his dark eyes flashing with fire.

Lauren ducked low on Twilight's back but not before she had caught sight of Dan staring at Twilight in horror. His mouth gaped open.

'*Arghhhhhhhh!*' he yelled in terror, as Twilight bore down on him.

The unicorn swooped upwards, missing him by centimetres, and disappeared into the darkness of the woods. He landed quietly.

Dan was still yelling and now the

other boys were shouting too. There was
the sound of the rope ladder being let
down. Lauren clutched Twilight's neck,
gulping back her laughter as she
remembered Dan's horrified face when he
had seen Twilight appear out of the sky.

'What's up?' she heard Nick shouting
to Dan as he clambered down the ladder.

'It was . . . it came through the sky at
me . . . big horn . . . galloping!' Dan
shouted.

'What came at you?' Lauren heard
Andrew demand.

'It was a uni– ' Dan broke off as if he
couldn't believe what he had seen with
his own eyes. 'It was a horse,' he said
quickly. 'A great white flying horse.'

'A flying horse!' Nick and Andrew exclaimed.

'With someone riding it,' Dan gasped. 'It came out of the sky. It just galloped straight at me. I couldn't see the person's head. Just their legs.'

'You mean a headless horseman?' Andrew laughed. 'Like a ghost!'

'Yeah!' Dan said, agreeing quickly. 'Yeah, that's what it was – it was a ghost!'

Nick and Andrew both laughed loudly.

'As if,' Nick said.

An idea filled Lauren's mind. 'Gallop round!' she said to Twilight. 'Make the sound of hoofbeats. Let's make them think there really *is* a headless horseman!'

Twilight didn't need telling twice.

Pricking up his ears, he started to canter through the bushes around the tree house, stamping his feet down as hard as he could.

'Listen!' Dan cried. 'There it is again!'

'Hey, you're right. I can see it!' Nick said, suddenly sounding frightened. 'Look – it's moving through the trees.'

'I can see it too!' cried Andrew.

Whinnying loudly, Twilight started cantering directly for the tree house. The sound of his hoofbeats seemed to fill the forest as he galloped down the path.

'*Arghhhhhhh!*' all three boys shouted in fright. 'It's a ghost – a real ghost!' And the next minute, Lauren saw them running off through the woods, falling over tree

roots and stumbling over stones in their
panic. Still yelling, they disappeared out
of sight.

Twilight stopped. 'We did it!'

Lauren's face split in a grin of astonishment and delight. They'd actually scared the boys away.

Twilight tossed his mane proudly. 'I must have looked really frightening.'

'I reckon you did,' Lauren smiled, hugging him. 'You were great.'

'It was your idea,' Twilight said.

'They were so scared,' Lauren laughed. 'Serves them right.'

Twilight snorted in a way that made it sound very much as if he was laughing too. 'Somehow I don't think they'll be coming back here in a hurry.'

Lauren patted his neck. 'I think you're right. Come on, let's go.'

As Twilight rose into the sky, Lauren frowned. 'I wonder if Nick's spelling book is still in the tree house,' she said. 'He'll get into trouble if he goes to school and says he's lost it.'

Part of her thought that Nick Snyder deserved all the trouble he got, but then she told herself not to be mean. He'd had enough of a fright without getting into trouble at school as well. 'Let's find it for him,' she said.

Twilight flew to the window. 'You know,' Lauren said, as she climbed inside to get Nick's book, 'this is going to make a great place for everyone to come and play. Now the boys have left it, everyone will be able to use it.' She reappeared with Nick's school book.

'So it looks like we've done two good deeds, after all,' Twilight said.

Lauren paused on the window ledge. 'I guess we have.'

They looked at each other. Neither of them spoke, but Lauren was sure she knew what Twilight was thinking. Had they just brought the time when he was going to leave her even closer?

The happiness that had been fizzing through her suddenly faded away.

She climbed slowly on to his back and they set off in an unhappy silence.

They were almost back at Granger's Farm when Lauren saw someone in the woods. 'It's Mrs Fontana and

Walter,' she said.

Twilight landed beside the old lady
and the terrier.

'Hello again,' Mrs Fontana said, smiling
at them. 'Where have you two been?'

'We've been at the creek scaring away
some boys who'd been pretending the
tree house was haunted,' Lauren replied
in a subdued voice.

Mrs Fontana noticed her sadness. 'What's
the matter? You don't sound very happy.'

Lauren looked at the ground. Twilight
hung his head.

'What is it?' Mrs Fontana said with
concern.

The words came tumbling out of
Lauren's mouth. 'Oh, Mrs Fontana,' she

answered unhappily, 'I don't know what to do. The more we help people, the sooner Twilight will have to go back to Arcadia. I want to do good but I don't want him to leave.'

'But the amount of good you do doesn't affect when Twilight leaves,' Mrs Fontana said in surprise.

'It doesn't?' Lauren said.

'No, my dear,' Mrs Fontana replied, shaking her head. 'You must have misunderstood me. Twilight will be with you for as long as you want him to be. It's up to you when he leaves.'

'I . . . I don't understand,' Lauren stammered in confusion.

Mrs Fontana took hold of her hands.

'One day, you will grow up and no longer need Twilight, Lauren,' she said, her bright eyes looking into Lauren's face. '*That* will be the day when the time has come for Twilight to go – and if he's done enough good deeds, then he'll become a Golden Unicorn.'

'But I'll always need Twilight,' Lauren exclaimed. Her eyes lit up with hope. 'Does that mean he can stay with me forever, Mrs Fontana?'

'He will stay for as long as you need him,' Mrs Fontana repeated softly.

Lauren looked at Twilight with delight. 'Then everything's OK.' She put her arms round his neck and hugged him close. 'You won't ever have to go away,

Twilight.' She turned to Mrs Fontana.
'We'll be together forever!'

A look full of wisdom and sadness
seemed to cross the old lady's face.
'Maybe,' she murmured.

Walter woofed and glanced down the

path. Mrs Fontana smiled and pulled her yellow shawl around her shoulders. 'I must go. Goodnight.'

'Goodnight,' Lauren replied.

Mrs Fontana started to walk away, then paused and looked back. 'The time you have together is precious,' she said softly, her bright eyes flickering intently from Lauren to Twilight. 'Make the most of it, my dears.'

Nine

'Lauren! Wait for me!'

Lauren turned on her way in through the school gates the next morning and saw Mel running towards her.

'Hi there,' Lauren said, waiting for her.

'Hi!' Mel said. She looked around. 'Where's Max? Isn't he coming to school today?'

'He's over there,' Lauren said. Max had run on ahead and was already playing ball with his friends. He was laughing and shouting happily.

'Do you want to go for a ride this afternoon?' Mel asked as she and Lauren continued into school.

'Yeah,' Lauren said.

Just then, Nick, Andrew and Dan came cycling past them. Lauren looked at them closely. Their faces were pale.

'Uh-oh,' Mel said, seeing them. 'Max and his friends had better watch out.'

Lauren watched the boys get off their bikes. 'If we go for a ride, we could go down to the creek again,' she said to Mel. She raised her voice so that the boys could hear. 'I want to explore that tree house.'

She saw Mel look at her with astonishment, but her attention was focused on the three boys. At the mention of the words *tree house* they swung round and stared at her.

'The tree house by the creek!' Dan said, looking scared. 'Don't go there – it's haunted!'

'By a headless horseman,' Andrew put in, coming over. 'He was there last night.'

'We saw him,' Dan told them. 'It was horrible!'

Mel's eyes widened with alarm. 'Really?'

'Yeah,' Nick said earnestly. 'I am never

going near that tree house again.' He looked at Lauren. 'I wouldn't go there if I were you.'

'I see,' Lauren said innocently.

The boys started to walk off.

'By the way, Nick,' Lauren called. She rummaged in her bag. 'Is this yours?' As she spoke, she held out Nick's book.

Nick came over. Taking it, he checked the inside cover and then stared at her. 'Yes. How did *you* get it?'

Lauren spoke coolly. 'Oh, I found it when I went to the tree house last night.'

She had to bite back a grin as all three boys and Mel stared at her as if she'd just gone crazy.

'*You* went to the tree house last night?'

Nick exclaimed.

'You couldn't have – we were there until it was dark,' Andrew said.

'I went *after* it was dark,' Lauren said.

'Did you see the headless horseman?' Dan demanded.

'I didn't,' Lauren said. She smiled cheerfully. 'But I promise I'll let you guys know if I see him *next* time I'm there.'

She took Mel's arm and smiled sweetly at them. 'See you then,' she said to the boys and, enjoying the speechless looks on their faces, she pulled Mel away.

Rounding a corner out of sight of the boys, Lauren burst out laughing.

Mel stared at her in astonishment. 'OK,' she said, breaking away and putting her hands on her hips. 'What *is* going on?'

Lauren grinned. 'It's a long story. Let's find Jessica and I'll tell you all about it.'

'I am *so* glad this place isn't haunted,' Jessica said as she, Lauren and Mel made themselves at home in the tree house after school. Below them, Shadow and

Twilight were grazing by the creek. 'Now everyone can share it and have fun.'

'Yeah,' Mel agreed, looking around as if she could hardly believe it. 'It'll be great!' She shook her head. 'So, tell us again,' she said to Lauren. 'You rode here and scared Nick and the others by galloping around on Twilight and pretending to be a ghost?'

For about the fiftieth time, Lauren nodded and told the story. 'I heard the boys here after school talking about scaring people and I saw them do it. I knew it wasn't haunted then, so I came back later with Twilight.' She crossed her fingers as she stretched the truth slightly.

'I wore a sheet
and pretended to be a ghost. Because
it was dark, Nick and the others
couldn't see Twilight properly through
the trees and they thought I was a real
ghost – a headless horseman.'

'That's incredible!' Jessica said.

'It was really brave of you to come here on your own at night,' Mel said admiringly to Lauren, 'even if you knew this place wasn't haunted.'

Lauren looked out of the window at Twilight grazing below. 'But I wasn't on my own,' she said, smiling. 'I had Twilight.'

my Secret Unicorn

When Lauren recites a secret spell, her pony
Twilight turns into a beautiful unicorn with magical
powers! Together Lauren and Twilight learn how to
use their magic to help their friends.

The Magic Spell
Linda Chapman

Dreams Come True
Linda Chapman

Flying High
Linda Chapman

Starlight Surprise
Linda Chapman

Stronger Than Magic
Linda Chapman

Look out for more **my Secret Unicorn** adventures

My Secret Unicorn

Most of the time, Twilight looks like an ordinary grey pony, but when Lauren says the words of a spell he transforms into a magical unicorn and together they can fly all over the world . . .

The Magic Spell
Linda Chapman

Look out for more **My Secret Unicorn** adventures

My Secret Unicorn

Lauren's nervous about starting a new school and making new friends. Can Twilight's magical powers help?

Look out for more **My Secret Unicorn** adventures

My Secret Unicorn

Lauren's friend Jessica is finding life at home
difficult. Lauren and Twilight want to help her but
can they persuade her to trust them?

Look out for more **My Secret Unicorn** adventures

My Secret Unicorn

On one of their evening fly-arounds Twilight starts to feel ill and he and Lauren have to stop exploring and return home. Can they find something stronger than magic to help Twilight get bettter. . .?

Look out for more *My Secret Unicorn* adventures